YUMA COUNTY LIBRARY DISTRICT

PROTECT YOURSELF ONLINE

THE RISKS OF SOCIAL MEDIA

by Janine Ungvarsky

BrightPoint Press

San Diego, CA

© 2022 BrightPoint Press
an imprint of ReferencePoint Press, Inc.
Printed in the United States

For more information, contact:
BrightPoint Press
PO Box 27779
San Diego, CA 92198
www.BrightPointPress.com

ALL RIGHTS RESERVED.

No part of this work covered by the copyright hereon may be reproduced or used in any form or by any means—graphic, electronic, or mechanical, including photocopying, recording, taping, web distribution, or information storage retrieval systems—without the written permission of the publisher.

LIBRARY OF CONGRESS CATALOGING-IN-PUBLICATION DATA

Names: Ungvarsky, Janine, author.
Title: The risks of social media / by Janine Ungvarsky.
Description: San Diego, CA : BrightPoint Press, [2022] | Series: Protect yourself online | Includes bibliographical references and index. | Audience: Grades 7-9
Identifiers: LCCN 2021040253 (print) | LCCN 2021040254 (eBook) | ISBN 9781678202521 (hardcover) | ISBN 9781678202538 (eBook)
Subjects: LCSH: Social media--Juvenile literature. | Cyberbullying--Juvenile literature. | Internet and children--Juvenile literature.
Classification: LCC HM742 .U77 2022 (print) | LCC HM742 (eBook) | DDC 302.23/1--dc23
LC record available at https://lccn.loc.gov/2021040253
LC eBook record available at https://lccn.loc.gov/2021040254

CONTENTS

AT A GLANCE	4
INTRODUCTION KALA'S STORY	6
CHAPTER ONE WHAT ARE THE RISKS OF SOCIAL MEDIA?	12
CHAPTER TWO SOCIAL MEDIA MAKES THE NEWS	26
CHAPTER THREE LOOKING OUT FOR TROUBLE ONLINE	42
CHAPTER FOUR PROTECTING YOURSELF ON SOCIAL MEDIA	60
Glossary	74
Source Notes	75
For Further Research	76
Index	78
Image Credits	79
About the Author	80

AT A GLANCE

- Social media can be fun. But there are also risks.

- Cyberbullies threaten or harass others on social media.

- Victims of cyberbullying may experience stress, anxiety, and other problems. They may even consider taking their own life.

- Hate speech means intimidating or insulting someone. It can be because of race, religion, or other parts of who the person is. Hate speech can spread widely on social media.

- Many people have blamed hate speech for the rise in hate crimes against Black people, Asian Americans, and immigrants.

- Fake news is false information that is presented as if it were true. Social media makes it easy for fake news to reach a large audience.

- Anyone using social media can fall victim to the risks that these platforms pose.

- Social media companies have taken some actions to fight these problems.

- Social media users can also protect themselves. Learning what the risks are is important.

- There are resources available to help teens protect themselves on social media.

INTRODUCTION

KALA'S STORY

Kala had just turned thirteen. She was finally old enough to sign up for social media. Lots of her friends already had profiles. Kala could not wait to see their posts and share her own.

She made her profile and posted her first selfie. Later, she was happy to see so many friends liked her picture. But one girl posted mean comments. Mia was an older girl Kala

Social media makes it easy to spread insults and embarrassing comments about other people.

knew from band. She made fun of Kala's weight and how her band uniform fit.

Kala told Mia to stop. But things only got worse. Mia got some of her friends to make fun of Kala too. Kala did not know what to

When young people are cyberbullied, they should talk to a parent or another trusted adult. They can help stop the cyberbullying.

do. She did not tell anyone what was going on, and Mia kept making fun of her.

After a couple of weeks, things got even worse. Mia posted that Kala sold the answers to tests. It was not true, but kids still started asking her to sell them answers. Kala was so afraid of getting in trouble she did not want to go to school. She felt sick to her stomach.

The principal heard what the kids were saying. He wanted to meet with Kala's mother. Kala finally told her about the posts.

Her mom said that sharing mean, false, or intimidating messages online is called cyberbullying. She told Kala it was not her fault. Then she told the principal. He addressed it with Mia and her parents. The cyberbullying stopped.

CYBER RISKS

What happened to Kala happens to many teens. A 2018 Pew Research Center survey reported that 59 percent of American teenagers had been cyberbullied. Many experienced anxiety, depression, and other problems because of it.

Social media can be a fun way for people to share information and photos. But it is also easy for people to share false or fake information. It can be used to say mean or hateful things. It can also be used to intimidate people online. Cyberbullying, hate speech, and fake news are some of the

Victims of cyberbullying can experience depression or other problems. It is important for them to reach out for help.

risks of using social media. But there are ways for teens to protect themselves from these risks.

CHAPTER ONE

WHAT ARE THE RISKS OF SOCIAL MEDIA?

Social media has its roots in the 1980s. True social media networks existed by the late 1990s. They became even more popular in the 2000s. These services make it easy for people to keep in touch. But people soon learned social media also created problems.

Cyberbullies use social media to spread lies or make fun of others. Sometimes they may threaten or try to intimidate their victim.

People sometimes say and do things on social media that they would not do in person. Bullying, hate speech, and fake news existed before social media. But social media made these things easier to do.

CYBERBULLYING

A bully **harasses**, threatens, or intimidates someone. A cyberbully uses an electronic device to do the same thing. Most cyberbullying happens on social media. The invention of social media gave bullies a new tool. They can bully anyone from anywhere.

Posting mean or false information about someone is an example of cyberbullying. So is sharing true information that is embarrassing. Making fun of something that someone did is called shaming. It is also cyberbullying. Posting threats to hurt someone is cyberbullying too.

Some cyberbullies make fake accounts. They pretend to be someone else. Then they post things to embarrass a person or get them in trouble. Others post embarrassing pictures. This sometimes happens when a dating couple breaks up.

ALL POSTS ARE PUBLIC

Oversharing is another social media risk. Oversharing is posting information that should be kept private. Posting revealing photos is an example of oversharing. Social media is public. Posts can be shared or saved. People can see them even if the original post is deleted. College recruiters and employers often review social media posts. A good rule is to assume anything posted can be seen by anyone at any time.

Girls are cyberbullied on social media more often than boys. They are more likely to bully others online as well.

Posting nude or sexual pictures of a former partner is called revenge porn. Many states have laws against revenge porn. It is also illegal to send or receive sexual photos of a person under age 18.

Girls are more likely to be victims of cyberbullies than boys. They are also more likely to be the bully. LGBTQ+ teens are four times more likely to be bullied than heterosexual teens. They are also more likely to be bullied more than once.

Henrietta Fore is the executive director of the United Nations Children's Fund. She said, "All over the world, young people . . . are telling us that they are being bullied online, that it is affecting their education, and that they want it to stop."[1]

HATE SPEECH

Hate speech can be a kind of cyberbullying. It is threatening, intimidating, or insulting someone because of who the person is.

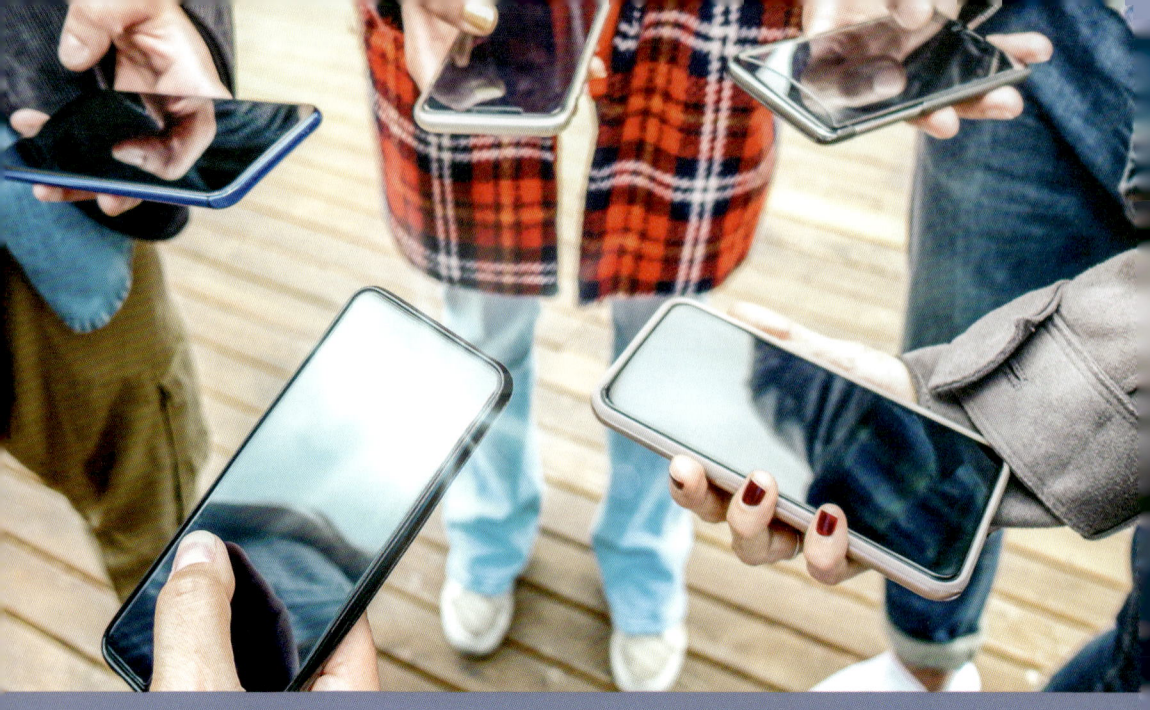

Hate speech can be spread quickly by social media to a large number of people.

It may be based on race, ethnicity, religion, or national origin. It can also be based upon disability, sexual orientation, or gender. Social media did not create hate speech. But it made hate speech easier to spread.

Hate speech can appear in personal posts. Sometimes it is in cartoons or memes that are easily shared. Hate speech can also be in videos or other content shared on social media.

Most hate speech is based on race, ethnicity, or national origin. Overall, more boys experience hate speech online. Girls are more likely to experience hate speech based on gender.

Black and Hispanic people are the most common victims of online hate speech. But other people can also be targeted. A 2020 Nielsen study found a spike in hate speech against Asian Americans. It increased by 145 percent that year. People wrongly

Asian Americans became a target of hate speech during the COVID-19 pandemic. Some people falsely blamed them for the coronavirus.

blamed them for the COVID-19 pandemic. The virus behind the pandemic was first seen in China.

Hate speech on social media can lead to violence. People make pages to share hateful speech. Sometimes they move from online hate speech to real-life attacks. They target the group they hate with vandalism or physical violence.

FAKE NEWS

Fake news is news presented as true even though it is not. The details make the story sound more exciting than it is. Many times,

SOCIAL MEDIA IS NOT REAL LIFE

Social media often creates unrealistic expectations. People post about happy events like awards and vacations. They may not post about negative experiences. This can make it look like their lives are better than they really are. Sometimes teens get depressed about this. It's important to remember that social media only shows what people choose to post. It is not what life is really like.

People often post photos online about vacations and other fun events. But social media is not a true reflection of everyday life.

the articles have sensational headlines to attract attention.

Fake news can occur on television and radio, and in newspapers and magazines. But it is especially common on social media. One reason for this is **anonymity**. People can hide their identity. They can post something without any proof it is true. And it's easy to share things on social media. The false information spreads quickly.

People create fake news to influence other people's views. They may want to change how others vote or shop. They may want to change people's opinions on social issues. Businesses might create fake news about other companies to hurt their business. Or someone may post fake information about another individual to make the person look bad. This information can seem real. It might even have some truth in it. But it is meant to mislead.

Almost anyone can fall for a fake news story. It is human nature to be interested in something exciting. Fake news stories are written to be exciting. People also believe fake news because it supports a view they already have. This is called confirmation bias.

People sometimes believe a fake story on social media because someone they know shared it. "We come across information, it makes us feel emotional, we get upset about it, we think other people should have this information," said Chrysalis Wright, PhD. "So, we share it, we like it, we send it to all

Social media can be a great way to keep in touch with family and friends. Users need to be aware of the risks involved so they can avoid them.

of our friends and family and then . . . the cycle just continues."[2]

Cyberbullying, hate speech, and fake news can make social media a risky place to be. But it does not have to be that way. Learning how to identify these problems can keep social media a fun place to connect with friends and family.

CHAPTER TWO

SOCIAL MEDIA MAKES THE NEWS

Technology was different in the 1990s compared to what we know today. Home computers used a phone line to get online. Websites could take 30 seconds to load. Cell phones did not connect to the internet or take pictures. They could only call and text. People only used social media on computers.

Online gaming became widely popular in the early 2000s. Social media is now an important part of gaming.

Technology improved rapidly in the 2000s. Wireless internet and phones that could connect to it were invented. People could post photos online. They could use social media anywhere. They could also play games, watch videos, and see ads.

   Before long, people found ways to misuse and abuse social media. Bullies did not have to find their victims in person. They could bother their victims anywhere and anytime online. More people could see what

SOCIAL MEDIA CHANGES THE NEWS

Social media changed how people get the news. People sign up to follow pages on social media. They may pick sites that post things they like. This affects the news they get. They do not get all the facts. People also tend to read the headlines and look at pictures. They may not read all the details.

bullies said too. Hateful speech and fake news could be shared easily and quickly.

CYBERBULLYING AND ONLINE SHAMING LEADS TO SUICIDES

The first American anti-bullying laws were passed in 1999. They came after an April 1999 school shooting at Columbine High School in Littleton, Colorado. People thought the shooters attacked because they were bullied.

Early laws mostly dealt with physical bullying. But cyberbullying started to make the news. In 2006, thirteen-year-old Megan Meier died by suicide. She was

Cyberbullying causes a great deal of pain to its victims. Some have even died by suicide.

upset because of fake posts on MySpace. The case shocked the world. It also drew attention to cyberbullying on social media.

Other cases followed. In 2008, Jessica Logan's ex-boyfriend shared pictures of her naked. Name-calling and bullying on social media followed. A few months later, she took her own life. She was eighteen. Then in 2009, thirteen-year-old Hope Stillwell sent a picture of her breasts to her boyfriend. Someone else shared the photo. When she was bullied on MySpace, Stillwell took her own life as well.

All of these tragic cases drew attention to cyberbullying. But the problem continued. One reason was how easy it was for posts to go **viral**. Viral posts get a lot of attention. Many people see them. They spread from one social media site to others. In the

When social media posts go viral, private or embarrassing information about the victim is shared with many people.

2010s, viral videos led to more anti-bullying laws. In 2011, New Jersey enacted a new antibullying law. This was passed in the wake of Tyler Clementi's death. He was a college student who jumped from a bridge because of a viral video of him kissing another man. This shaming incident cost him his life. A federal law named after Clementi has also been proposed. It would require colleges and universities to have an anti-harassment policy.

HATE SPEECH THEN AND NOW

The problems of hate speech were known long before social media. Organizations like the Anti-Defamation League worked against it in the early 1900s. The National Association for the Advancement of Colored People did as well. The **anti-Semitism** of Germany's Nazi government in the 1940s drew attention to hate speech against Jews. Hate speech continues to be a problem today.

Social media creates new ways to spread hate speech. Posts are not limited to words. They can have images and videos. Studies have shown that posts with images get 350 percent more likes, comments, and shares than posts without them. When someone posts a picture that makes fun of someone's race or religion, many people may see it.

Most social media companies do not want hate speech on their sites. People

Hate speech often targets people of a specific race or religion.

do not like it. Businesses sometimes stop advertising if they think a site is allowing it. In August 2020, Facebook founder Mark Zuckerberg told Congress that hate speech "hurts our business."[3]

Hate crimes increased in the US during 2020, especially against Black people. Many people blame hate speech for encouraging these crimes.

The companies try to stop hate speech. They block some posts and users. Some people complain this is **censorship**. In the United States, the Constitution promises freedom of speech. But this applies to the government restricting speech. Social media companies are private businesses. They can make their own rules.

These rules were in the news often between 2017 and 2021. During Donald Trump's term as president, some of his posts were blocked. So were posts from many of his supporters. Social media companies said the posts had hate speech or incited violence. Many of these posts and tweets had insulted Asian Americans, Black people, and immigrants. Trump was later banned from Twitter, Facebook, Instagram, and YouTube.

FAKE NEWS: OLD PROBLEM, NEW TWIST

Fake news has been a problem as long as there has been news. At least as far back as the 1600s, some newspapers twisted or bent the truth. The difference was it was not always called fake news.

TIKTOK TRIUMPH

TikTok has become a true social media success. Its user numbers have exploded since its start in 2016. As of 2021, the app has about 689 million users each month. About 62 percent of its users are between ten and twenty-nine years old. Most social media apps build on connections users have with others. TikTok instead focuses on content. Like other types of social media, its content includes news stories.

Many people get their news by scrolling through their Facebook or Twitter feeds.

The term *fake news* is credited to BuzzFeed editor Craig Silverman. In 2014, he saw some websites that looked like real news sites, but they had made-up news. Silverman called them fake news sites.

The term became popular in January 2017. Then-president Trump said some

People often share posts on social media to express ideas they believe. They hope to persuade others to agree with them.

legitimate news sites had fake news.

Trump's critics said the president only said this because he didn't like the reporting. From then on, some people used the term *fake news* to mean news they did not like.

Some people ignore news they do not agree with. They share only news they want to believe. And because social media makes it so easy to share things, fake news travels faster than ever. Some platforms also send users more of the same information they've read or liked. So the same news gets repeated, even if it is fake.

CHAPTER THREE

LOOKING OUT FOR TROUBLE ONLINE

A 2021 study by the Pew Research Center showed that 84 percent of teens use social media. There are many good things about social media. Teens connect, learn, and have fun on social media sites. These services give teens an easy way to interact with their friends online.

Almost 60 percent of teens in the United States have encountered abuse online.

But social media also exposes teens to risks. A 2018 Pew survey found that 59 percent of US teens have experienced abusive behavior online. This includes threats, false rumors, and name-calling. It also includes sending explicit photos of the person without his or her consent. Hate speech and fake news are common. Knowing what these risks look like makes them easier to avoid.

WHEN IS IT CYBERBULLYING?

Most cyberbullies send harassing messages or posts. They make fun of the victim or share things that are not true. This is called cyberstalking.

Some cyberbullies exclude their victim. They post mean things or lies but do not let the victim see them. Other bullies post things that are true but that the victim does not want people to know. For example,

Some bullies pretend to be someone else online. They hide behind this fake identity so their victim doesn't know who's harassing them.

a teen might be gay but not ready to tell anyone. When the bully shares that information, it is called an outing.

Masquerading is also cyberbullying. Masquerading is when the bully pretends to be someone else. The bully makes a fake account or uses someone else's real account to hide his or her identity. Sometimes a bully takes over the victim's account. The bully pretends to be the victim. Then the bully sends messages that embarrass the victim or get the victim in trouble. There is usually a power difference between the cyberbully and the victim. For example, the bully may be older or a sports

BULLYING VS. CYBERBULLYING

Cyberbullying is more public that bullying because anyone can see social media posts. It is harder to escape because social media can be anywhere. Cyberbullying lasts longer because posts never really disappear. And it is harder for adults to see it happening unless they check the teen's social media.

Cyberbullying follows a victim whenever or wherever they use social media.

team captain. This makes the victim afraid to tell anyone.

One important part of cyberbullying is that it is intentional. In other words, the bully is not just teasing. He or she wants to upset or embarrass the victim. For example, a

Cyberbullying victims become very upset about being bullied. The experience may cause stress, anxiety, and other problems.

bully could share video of someone spilling his or her lunch tray and everyone laughing at the person. The bully also does not stop if asked.

A good way to identify cyberbullying is by how the victim feels. Victims will be very upset about the bullying. They may feel stressed and anxious. They might feel embarrassed or ashamed. They may feel very angry, but they also think they cannot do anything about it. Bullied teens may get stomachaches and headaches. They may not want to go to school. They may feel like taking their own life. Social media posts that make a teen feel this way are cyberbullying.

HATE SPEECH OR FREE SPEECH?

Online hate speech can be a form of cyberbullying. Someone posting comments making fun of someone because of his or her race, gender, or another **protected characteristic** is bullying. But hate speech can go beyond cyberbullying. It can be aimed at whole groups of people. Hate speech can also be used to encourage others to attack these groups.

Hate speech can be hard to define. People use social media to share their views. It can be hard to decide what is free speech and what is hate speech. Two things can help identify hate speech. One is the context of a comment. The other is its intent. Context means the words and thoughts around something. Words and phrases have different meanings depending on where and how they are used.

Hate speech can take many forms. Sometimes the words used can even encourage violence.

For example, tattletales are sometimes called rats. It's not nice, but it is not hate speech. But in the 1930s, Nazis referred to Jewish people as rats. They wanted to make them seem less than human. This was hate speech. "Context is so important. It's critical when we are looking to determine whether or not something is hate speech, or a credible threat of violence," said Monika Bickert, Facebook's head of policy.[4]

Intent is what people meant their words to do. Referring to a person as gay is not hate speech if the person is okay with others knowing this. But if someone calls a person gay to embarrass or threaten him or her, it is hate speech.

Identifying hate speech can be tricky. But posts intended to embarrass or hurt someone because of his or her race, religion, or other protected characteristic

People have a tendency to believe what they want to be true. This is one reason why it can be difficult to identify fake news.

are probably hate speech. Posts that encourage others to try to hurt the person for these reasons are also hate speech.

HOW FAKE IS FAKE NEWS?

Identifying fake news can be hard. The people who make it are sometimes good at making it seem real. And people like to believe what they want to be true. This is called confirmation bias. People tend to favor information that confirms their beliefs.

Even the experts find fake news hard to fight. "While working to fix it, we've been accused of apathy, censorship, political bias, and optimizing for our business and share price instead of the concerns of society," said Twitter cofounder Jack Dorsey. "This is not who we are, or who we ever want to be."[5]

Fake news takes on different forms. Some is more dangerous than others. But all of it can cause problems. Sometimes

Saturday Night Live is an example of a TV show that uses satire both to entertain people and to make them think.

fake news is simply a mistake. A reporter could get a fact wrong in an article. Social media helps it spread quickly. Even if it is fixed, the people who saw the original story might still believe the fake news.

Some fake news is satire. Satire uses humor to criticize something. It is written to entertain people and make them think. Satire is not meant to mislead, but sometimes it does. For example, a piece of satire about a politician who opposes construction projects may claim he even wants to ban toy building blocks. This is meant to poke fun. But if people do not realize that, they may think it is true.

Clickbait stories are another form of fake news. The headline is deliberately misleading. This tricks people into looking at the story. Often the news creator earns more advertising money if many people click on the story. But if people only read the headline, they are not getting true news.

Clickbait stories are usually exaggerated. They are designed to grab people's attention.

Propaganda and disinformation are the most serious kinds of fake news. These are stories that are intentionally untrue. They are meant to mislead people. This is usually done for political or financial reasons. The stories are often written to make people want to share them. Social media makes this easy and helps the stories spread fast.

There are many types of risks to be found on social media. Cyberbullying and hate speech can hurt people. Fake news can affect important things like how people

PEANUT BUTTER CUPS PANIC

Many fake news stories focus on politics or health matters. But fake news can be about any topic—even candy! In 2017, a fake news story appeared about Reese's Peanut Butter Cups. The story said the candy would no longer be sold. The story went viral on Facebook. It generated more than 820,000 shares, comments, and reactions in just four days. People were shocked and upset. Fortunately for candy lovers, the news was fake.

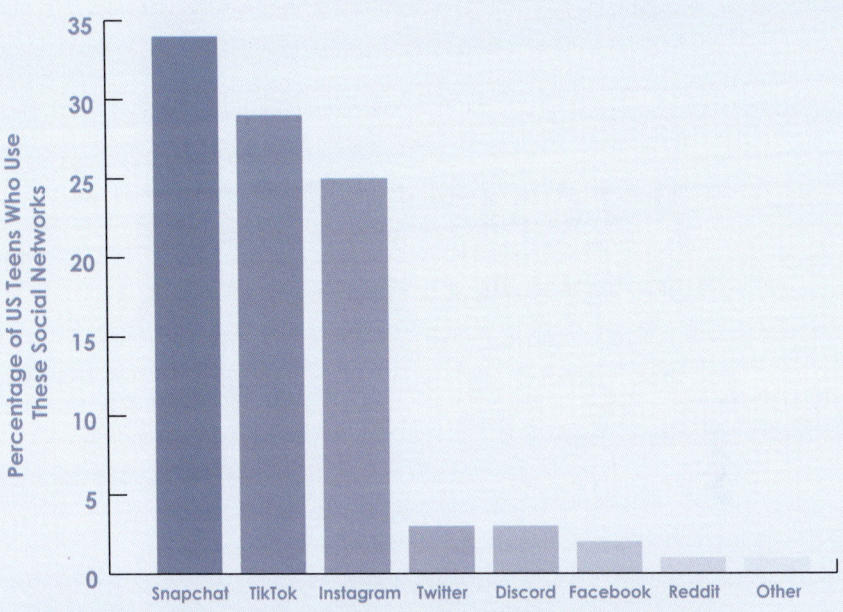

Source: "Most Popular Social Networks of Teenagers in the United States from Fall 2012 to Fall 2020," Statista, October 2020. www.statista.com.

Snapchat, TikTok, and Instagram were by far the most popular social media platforms used by US teens in fall 2020.

spend money and vote. Being aware of what these risks look like can help teens be ready to respond when they find them.

CHAPTER FOUR

PROTECTING YOURSELF ON SOCIAL MEDIA

Anyone can be a victim of social media risks, even people who do not use social media. A cyberbully can use his or her own account to attack a victim. A group stirred up by online hate speech can vandalize property anywhere. And friends can share fake news without realizing it.

Cyberbullying is never the fault of the victim. It's important for victims to talk to a parent or another adult about the situation. They will be able to help.

The good news is there are ways to be safer on social media. There are places to turn for help too. It comes down to being aware, knowing when to share, and caring enough to help yourself and others.

DEFEATING CYBERBULLIES

Being picked on by a cyberbully feels awful. The mean posts are upsetting. It's humiliating to think about all the people who saw them. Cyberbully victims feel angry and powerless. They may want to stay home. These problems continue until the bullying stops.

One of the most important things a victim should do is to tell a parent or other adult. They will help stop the bullying. The victim can also take additional steps. He or she can directly tell the bully to stop. The victim should block the bully. Social media sites have ways to block others from seeing posts and other content. The bully should be reported to the social media site. He or she can also be reported to school officials and the police. The victim should keep copies of the posts and messages to help with reporting the bullying.

It is also important that teens who see someone being cyberbullied speak up.

EMBARRASSED TO ASK FOR HELP?

It is not always easy for teens involved in cyberbullying to ask for help. They may feel foolish or ashamed. They may be afraid of getting in trouble themselves. But getting help is important. If there is no adult to talk to, teens can look online for a helpline to call.

If someone is considering suicide, he or she should talk to someone. Counselors are available 24 hours a day at the National Suicide Prevention Lifeline.

They can tell the bully what they are doing is not okay. Friends of someone who is being bullied can also help by telling an adult. This is especially important if they think someone is in danger from physical harm or suicide. People can stand up for friends who are being bullied.

HALTING HATE SPEECH

Stopping online hate speech is hard. There are not many laws to help. But there are things that can be done to protect victims.

Hate speech directed at one person may be cyberbullying. If this is the case, the same methods can be used to help stop it.

SUICIDE PREVENTION

Fear, anger, and embarrassment are very powerful emotions. They affect how people think. If someone is considering ending their life, call the National Suicide Prevention Lifeline at 1-800-273-8255. As of July 16, 2022, this number will be shortened to 988. Trained experts there can help. If someone is in immediate danger, call 911.

When people see hate speech—or any type of bullying—take place, they should stand up for the victim. They should tell the bully to stop.

Victims can report the posts to the social media site. They can remove posts or block the poster. Another thing they can do is to raise awareness. Hate speech does more than hurt feelings. It makes some people seem less important than others. Hate speech also encourages violence against the groups it is aimed at. Help family and friends understand its dangers. Everyone can stand up for people who are targets of hate speech. People can tell those who are using hate speech to stop. Sometimes they

WHAT IF I'M THE BULLY?

It might seem like teasing, but cyberbullying has real consequences. Schools have policies against cyberbullying even if it happens outside school. Bullies can be kicked out of school, sports teams, and clubs. And legal penalties are a real possibility. Plus, cyberbullies sometimes experience depression and physical illness from bullying, just like their victims.

People should always check the sources of news stories on social media to make sure they're from reputable sources.

do not realize that what they are posting hurts. This also helps hate speech targets feel supported.

People can also post and share messages of kindness and tolerance. This gives other people an alternative to hate speech to share. It also gives them a positive message to ponder.

OUTSMART FAKE NEWS

"It's increasingly hard to spot fake news stories in today's world," said psychologist Dr. Linda Papadopoulos. "Even reputable news organizations have found themselves reporting on fake stories in recent times."[6] News is now circulated online by an increasing number of media outlets. Scoops are revealed on Twitter and websites. TV networks announce breaking news around the clock. There is greater competition to report stories quickly. This puts an emphasis on speed. Sometimes this affects the quality of reporting.

There are ways people can identify fake news. First, check the source of the news. What is the poster's motive? Does that source usually support one view? Is it satire? Are the supporting facts from a reliable source? People should check the dates of articles and statistics used in them. Some sites post old articles. Others use facts from old articles. Things change. Be sure the news is current.

Sometimes headlines are misleading. They could be clickbait. The linked articles

Readers should take a close look at news stories to make sure they're not clickbait or old articles.

might say something different. There might be more facts behind the stories. Readers should also watch for misspelled words or other mistakes. This is a sign the story is not from a real news site. Readers should not share a story until they are sure it's true.

NO EASY SOLUTION

Social media companies have taken steps to stop cyberbullying, control hate speech, and limit fake news. They are also open to help. During a 2018 Congressional hearing, Facebook head Mark Zuckerberg said, "My position is not that there should be no [government] regulation. I think the real question . . . is what is the right regulation."[7]

Users need to know the risks and protect themselves. They should be careful about what they share online. They should

People should always be careful about sharing news articles on social media. They should confirm that the story is accurate before posting.

look out for others and ask for help when needed. This will help make social media the safe place for people to connect that it was meant to be.

GLOSSARY

anonymity

when someone's identity is unknown or hidden

anti-Semitism

hostility toward or discrimination against Jews as a religious, ethnic, or racial group

censorship

when someone in authority, like a government or company, stops something from being said or written because they do not like something about it

harasses

annoys or bothers someone over a period of time

propaganda

information that is meant to change someone's view; it is often not the whole truth about something

protected characteristic

a trait such as a person's race, religion, sexual orientation, or age; it is illegal to discriminate against people because of these traits

viral

a social media post that becomes very popular very quickly and is seen by thousands or millions of people

SOURCE NOTES

CHAPTER ONE: WHAT ARE THE RISKS OF SOCIAL MEDIA?

1. Quoted in "UNICEF Poll: More Than a Third of Young People in 30 Countries Report Being a Victim of Online Bullying," *UNICEF*, September 3, 2019. www.unicef.org.

2. Quoted in Vaile Wright, "Speaking of Psychology with Chrysalis Wright: Fake News and Why It Matters," *American Psychological Association*, August 2019. www.apa.org.

CHAPTER TWO: SOCIAL MEDIA MAKES THE NEWS

3. Quoted in Emily Czachor, "Facebook Removes Most Hate Speech Before People See It, Zuckerberg Tells Congress," *Newsweek*, July 29, 2020. www.newsweek.com.

CHAPTER THREE: LOOKING OUT FOR TROUBLE ONLINE

4. Quoted in Aarti Shahani, "From Hate Speech to Fake News," *NPR*, November 17, 2016. www.npr.org.

5. Quoted in Kaylee Fagan, "Twitter CEO Jack Dorsey Says 'We Aren't Proud of How People Have Taken Advantage of Our Service,'" *Insider*, March 1, 2018. www.businessinsider.com.

CHAPTER FOUR: PROTECTING YOURSELF ON SOCIAL MEDIA

6. Quoted in "Talking to Your Kids About Fake News," *Internet Matters*, January 26, 2021. www.internetmatters.org.

7. Quoted in Catherine Clifford, "Elon Musk Says Regulate Social Media: 'We Can't Have Willy-Nilly Proliferation of Fake News, That's Crazy,'" *CNBC*, April 11, 2018. www.cnbc.com.

FOR FURTHER RESEARCH

BOOKS

Jonathan Cristall, *What They Don't Teach Teens: Life Safety Skills for Teens and the Adults Who Care for Them*. Fresno, CA: Quill Driver Books, 2020.

Michael Miller, *Fake News: Separating Truth from Fiction*. Minneapolis, MN: Twenty-First Century Books, 2019.

Andrea C. Nakaya, *Social Media Hate Speech*. San Diego, CA: ReferencePoint Press, 2020.

INTERNET SOURCES

"Bullying and Cyberbullying," *Help Guide*, n.d. www.helpguide.org.

"Hate Speech Soars for Young Social Media Users," *Axios*, March 17, 2021. www.axios.com.

"How to Spot Fake News," *Cornell University*, July 14, 2021. http://guides.library.cornell.edu.

WEBSITES

Cyberbullying Research Center
www.cyberbullying.org

This research center website offers a wealth of resources about cyberbullying. It includes presentations, blogs, statistics, information on laws, and more for teens, parents, and educators.

Smart Social: Learn How to Shine Online
www.smartsocial.com

This website provides videos, speeches, and other resources for teens and their parents and educators to help teens be smart and safe while online.

STOMP Out Bullying: End the Hate . . . Change the Culture
www.stompoutbullying.org

This organization offers resources on cyberbullying, hate speech, and more for teens. This website includes a helpline and resources for teens experiencing bullying.

INDEX

anxiety, 10, 49

bullies, 14, 17, 28–29, 44–48, 62–64, 67
bullying, 13, 29, 31, 46, 48–49, 62–63, 67

clickbait, 56, 70
Columbine High School, 29
confirmation bias, 24, 54
COVID-19 pandemic, 20
cyberbullies, 14–16, 44, 46, 60, 62, 67
cyberbullying, 9–10, 14, 17, 25, 29–31, 44–50, 58, 63, 65, 67, 72
cyberstalking, 44

depression, 10, 67

ethnicity, 18–19

Facebook, 35, 37, 52, 58–59, 72
fake news, 10, 13, 21–25, 29, 38–39, 41, 44, 53–58, 60, 69–70, 72
freedom of speech, 36

gender, 18–19, 49

hate speech, 10, 13, 17–20, 25, 33–37, 44, 49–53, 58, 60, 65–69, 72

Instagram, 37, 59

masquerading, 45

National Suicide Prevention Lifeline, 65
Nazis, 33, 51

outing, 45
oversharing, 15

propaganda, 57
protected characteristic, 49, 52

race, 18–19, 34, 49, 52
religion, 18, 34, 52
revenge porn, 16

satire, 55–56, 70
sexual orientation, 18
shaming, 14, 33
Snapchat, 59
suicide, 29, 31, 33, 49, 64–65

TikTok, 38, 59
Trump, Donald, 37, 39, 41
Twitter, 37, 54, 59, 69

viral, 31–33, 58

Zuckerberg, Mark, 35, 72

IMAGE CREDITS

Cover: © SpeedKingz/Shutterstock Images
5: © damircudic/iStockphoto
7: © fizkes/iStockphoto
8: © Daisy Daisy/Shutterstock Images
11: © MIA Studio/Shutterstock Images
13: © SpeedKingz/Shutterstock Images
16: © VMJones/iStockphoto
18: © ViewApart/iStockphoto
20: © Chainarong Prasertthai/iStockphoto
22: © Vova Shevchuk/Shutterstock Images
25: © Monkey Business Images/Shutterstock Images
27: © Jennie Book/Shutterstock Images
30: © LightField Studios/Shutterstock Images
32: © Oleg Golovnev/Shutterstock Images
35: © aylinnn/iStockphoto
36: © Motortion/iStockphoto
39: © fizkes/iStockphoto
40: © Prostock-studio/Shutterstock Images
43: © SpeedKingz/Shutterstock Images
45: © Motortion Films/Shutterstock Images
47: © BongkarnGraphic/Shutterstock Images
48: © aslysun/Shutterstock Images
51: © asiandelight/Shutterstock Images
53: © Sylvie Bouchard/Shutterstock Images
55: © g0d4ather/Shutterstock Images
57: © Akhenaton Images/Shutterstock Images
59: © Red Line Editorial
61: © Motortion Films/Shutterstock Images
64: © Prostock-studio/Shutterstock Images
66: © Prostock-studio/Shutterstock Images
68: © McLittle Stock/Shutterstock Images
71: © kali9/iStockphoto
73: © Prostock-studio/Shutterstock Images

ABOUT THE AUTHOR

Janine Ungvarsky is former journalist who writes nonfiction for children and young adults.